Knife-edge

by

Robert Swindells

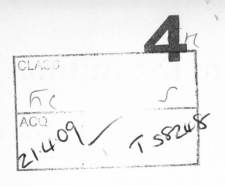

First published in 2008 in Great Britain by
Barrington Stoke Ltd
18 Walker Street, Edinburgh, EH3 7LP

www.barringtonstoke.co.uk

ISBN: 978-1-84299-541-9

Printed in Great Britain by Bell & Bain Ltd

A Note from the Author

What a sad bit of news. I couldn't believe it when I found out that they use in schools the same metal-detectors they use at airports. That's to stop pupils carrying knives. I was a teacher a long time ago and out of all the things that have changed in schools over the years, this has to be one of the saddest. I wrote this story because of how I felt.

Carrying a weapon does not keep the person who carries it safe. In America anyone can carry a gun. And what happens there is that hundreds of ordinary people die each year from gunshot wounds. There's an old saying – *he who lives by the gun will die by the gun.* The same is true for knives.

Only numpties carry knives.

For all who go unarmed

Contents

Chapter 1
Self Defence

Hey. Sam's my name. I'm 14. I go to Orwell School in Gretley. It's not bad, but there's a gang called the Landsharks. It's got ten guys in it, all well hard. Cecil True is the leader. Kids laugh at names like Cecil, but no one laughs at Cecil True. If they did, they'd never laugh again. At anything.

We went to the same primary school, Cecil and me. We were little. I didn't know Cecil was going to be a gang leader, did I? I laughed at his name. Every day. "Want to wrestle,

Cecil?" I'd say. I called him 'Cess the Mess' as well. Hard to believe now.

He hasn't forgotten. He doesn't say anything, but I know he remembers by the way he looks at me. He hasn't got time to get me for it just now. He's too busy. He's got gang stuff to do all the time. But one day, when he gets a spare minute, Cecil's going to get even. And I don't fancy that at all.

The Landsharks carry knives. They don't go round knifing people all the time. I'm not saying that. But everyone knows they carry knives, so everyone's scared of them.

I always walk home with my best mate. His name's Tim. We live in the same street. Prince Street. We don't hang about. We walk quickly, watching out for the Landsharks. There's a little park on our way home. Sparrow Park. It'd be nice to muck about in there, but we can't. We don't dare. Cecil says Sparrow Park's Landshark territory. If the gang catches some kid in there, they punch him up and take his phone. They pinch his watch and his cash as well. The Landsharks aren't there all the time, but it isn't worth the risk.

One tea-time, me and Tim are passing Sparrow Park and Tim says, "I've got a knife."

"Huh?" I look at him.

"A knife," he says. "Look."

He lifts his sweat-shirt. There's a great big knife stuck down the front of his trousers. He pulls it out so I can see the blade. It's long and wide and curvy. One edge has a row of pointy little teeth, a bit like a saw.

"Wow!" I gasp. "Where'd you get it?"

"Sports shop," he grins. "It's a fisherman's knife."

"I thought you had to be 18 to buy a knife," I say.

He nods. "You do. My cousin got it for me. He's 19."

"Let's have a look," I ask.

He hands me the knife. It's heavy. The blade glints in the sun. "Gonna start fishing, then?" I say.

Tim grins. "Sort of," he says. "Fishing for Landsharks."

My mouth drops open. "You're not gonna go after Cecil and them?" I gasp.

He shakes his head. "Not go *after*. But I'll get it out if they hassle me." He smiles. "Self defence."

I think about it later, at home. Self defence. No one can blame a guy for defending himself, can they? And if you've ever laughed at a guy like Cecil True, you'll *have* to defend yourself sooner or later. I think I need to get a knife of my own.

4

I shut myself in my room, go on the Internet. Type in the word *knives*. There's more than a *million* sites! I look at the first ten. They sell every sort of knife. Even swords from Japan – Samurai swords. One snag – *none* of them will sell to me. You've got to be 18 to buy from them. I say a bad word and come offline.

I don't have a cousin. Well, I *do*, but she's only seven. No use sending *her* in the sports shop to buy a knife for me. Have to think of some other way to get one.

I could pinch one of Mum's. A kitchen knife. She's got six, all different sizes. Trouble is, they hang in a row by the cooker. She'd notice in two seconds if one was missing.

I don't know what to do. As it happens, it'll be sorted soon by pure luck, but I don't know that. I lie awake half the night, trying to work something out.

Chapter 2
Other People's Rubbish

Orwell School has this course. Citizenship. It's about how to be a good citizen. You know. Don't bunk off school. Don't spray graffiti. Be polite. Don't drop litter. Help people.

Some of us go out two afternoons a week to do stuff for senior citizens. That means old people. We do decorating. Gardening. Fitting security chains on doors. Stuff like that. Our teacher, Mr Pringle, puts me with this really old guy called Jack Conyers. First time I knock on his door, old Jack gawps at me like I'm a ghost or something. "I'm Sam Brown," I says.

"From Orwell School? I've come to help do some jobs for you."

"Oh, aye," he says, when at last the message gets to his brain. "They *told* me someone'd be coming. Any good at digging, are you?"

I shrug. "Anyone can dig," I says. "Not rocket science, is it, Mr Conyers?" I'm thinking, *Is he going to let me in, or keep me standing on the step all afternoon?*

After a bit he decides I'm not a mugger. "You'd better come in," he says. "Sit down for a minute. D'you want a cup of tea?"

He's all right, old Conyers. We sit drinking tea. It's better than double maths anyway. He says he can still do most things in the garden, but not the heavy digging. That's going to be my job.

We finish the tea. Then we go outside. He points to a sad old shed. "You'll find all the tools in there," he tells me. "Just take anything you need."

The garden's like a flipping jungle. Tall weeds and high, clumpy grass. I keep thinking I'll see a tiger, or a herd of elephants. He shows me the part he wants dug. It's the same size as France. "Start with the fork," he says. "Easier than the spade."

He goes in the house. I go to the shed. It's full of stuff, you can hardly move. The fork and spade are near the front wall. There's a rake as well, and an old broom. At the back there's a saggy old side-board. There's loads of stuff all over it – big bags of seed, plant-pots, balls of string – you name it. Under the side-board are three drawers. I pull one open. *It's interesting*, I think, *I like snooping in other people's rubbish*. It's a really heavy drawer, with rusty tins full of nails, screws and bits of old metal. I scrabble about and shove stuff aside. It's dim in the shed, but right at the bottom something gleams, and that's how I find my knife.

I lift it out. Lay it on my hand. Stare at it. It's beautiful. I don't mean fancy. It doesn't glitter like Tim's fisherman's knife. In fact it's black all over – the blade and everything. There are no pointy teeth and it's not heavy. It's a slim dagger – a stiletto. Both the edges are sharp – very sharp. If I carry it in my waistband nothing'd show. But I'd have to be careful not to hurt myself with it.

I've already decided to nick it. Well, why not? It was right at the bottom of the drawer. Old Conyers hasn't touched it in years. Forgotten he's got it, I expect. It's a waste, leaving it lost under all that rusty stuff. And anyway, what would an old man like him do with a dagger? I slip it into an inside pocket of my jacket.

It's April. A warm day. It's hard work, digging. I'm sweating. I take off my jacket, hang it on the fence. *It'd cost Conyers a packet*, I tell myself, *to get this dug over by a gardener. All I'm getting is a rotten old knife.* It makes me feel better about nicking it.

He brings me a mug of tea. Looks at the turned soil, all the ground I've dug. Says, "Great job, Sam, keep up the good work." Goes back inside.

I dig till home time.

Chapter 3
Schoolboy Citizens

The day I start with Jack Conyers is a Tuesday. A big bunch of us are out, helping different grave-dodgers. Wednesday morning we have a meeting with Mr Pringle, or Crispy as we call him. He's in charge of the Citizenship project. Wants to know how we all got on.

"All right, Sam," he goes when it's my turn, "tell us what you did."

But I *can't*, can I? Think about it. *"It was warm work, sir, digging a plot the size of France, but I did manage to nick a really good knife. A stiletto. It's here, tucked down my trousers. I intend to cut Cecil True with it one of these days."*

Yeah, right. What I *actually* say is, "It was all right, sir. Bit warm. I did some digging. Mr Conyers said it was a great job. Can't wait to carry on, Thursday."

"Splendid, Sam," says Crispy, and rubs his hands together. It's all right for him. We do the work, and every old age pensioner in Gretley thinks *he's* a saint. Saint Crispy.

At morning break I catch Tim by the sports block. "Got your knife, have you, Tim?"

"'Course." He grins, pats the bump round his middle.

"Me too," I tell him. I whip up my sweat-shirt, pull out the knife. I'm close to the wall so other kids won't see.

Tim asks to hold it. I pass it to him.

"Hmmm," he goes, as he feels it in his hand, "light, isn't it? And sharp. Where'd you get it?"

"Took it off a mugger," I lie. "Last night in Sparrow Park."

"Yeah, right," Tim says. He hands it back. "You don't have to tell me if you don't want, you idiot."

"No." I shake my head. "Actually it was in the old guy's shed where I was working yesterday. He didn't want it any more."

Tim looked at me. "*Tell* you that, did he?"

"Not in so many words," I say, "but if you want something, you don't bury it under loads of rubbish, do you?"

Tea time, we walk home with our weapons well hidden. "Two years in jail," grunts Tim, "if a copper stops us."

"No copper will," I tell him. "Look at us. We're good schoolboy citizens, you and me."

After tea I go up to my room, shut the door. My family never comes in my room without banging on the door and asking first. I get out of uniform, pull on some jeans and a top. I tuck the knife down my jeans and face the mirror.

I practise quick draws. I spin round in a crouch, stabbing and slashing. I try out mean, nasty looks as well. I scowl. I show my teeth, narrow my eyes, stick out my tongue. Make faces like a New Zealand Maori doing the *haka*. I growl and look in the mirror to see. I don't know what it'll do to Cecil True, but it scares me right enough.

I start thinking about this girl. Suzi Pool. She's in my year at Orwell. She's drop-dead gorgeous. Sometimes I can hardly do my work for looking at her. I want to go with her, but she likes older guys. I once invited her to

Pulse for a coffee. It's cool, all the kids go there, but she's like, "Get lost, wimp – I don't date babies." *Babies*. It had taken me weeks to get up the nerve to ask her. I was gutted when she said that to me.

I feel so good after my practice session with the knife, I decide to phone Suzi. Maybe she'll be out with some smoothie from Year 11, but you never know your luck.

She picks up. I go, "Hi, Suzi, it's Sam."

"Sam who?" she says.

"Sam," I goes. "You know, at school?"

"Oh." She sounds so bored I nearly hang up. "What do you want?"

"Where are you?" I says.

She sighs. "At home, *why?*"

"Fancy a burger?"

"With you?"

"Sure, with me. You don't have to *marry* me or anything. We eat burgers, talk a bit, I walk you home. What d'you say?"

She doesn't say anything. It goes so quiet I think she's hung up. "Hello?" I goes.

"OK," she says. "See you outside Pulse in 20 minutes."

I'm so gob-smacked, I sit gawping at my phone instead of getting ready.

Chapter 4
Ten Feet Tall

I'm outside Pulse at seven in my hoodie, jeans, Nikes and hidden knife. No sign of Suzi. *It's cool*, I tell myself. *I'm early, and girls're always late.* I walk up and down, but not near the window. There are kids from school inside. If Suzi stands me up, I don't want them to know.

She shows up ten minutes late. She's wearing a sleeveless jacket over a crop top, a skirt so short it's really a belt, and boots. She doesn't say why she's late, so I don't ask. I can hardly believe she's come at all. We go in.

Everyone looks, like I knew they would. *Hey,* they're thinking, *look who's with Suzi Pool.* I'm ten feet tall.

We take a corner table. I pass Suzi the menu. "What'll you have?" I ask. She scans the card and takes her time. "The Health-in-a-bun," she says at last. "Apple juice to drink."

"Health-in-a-bun?" I hoot. "That's like, salad and bread. You could get that at home."

She gives a sigh and looks at me as if I'm stupid. "Do you like my shape, Sam?" she murmurs.

"'Course," I tell her. "What guy wouldn't?"

"Well," she goes. "I don't stay that way by scoffing super-size cheese-burgers and triple fries. Or drinking Cokes." She hands me the menu. "You have what you like."

I get a whopper and fries, jumbo banana shake. Nothing seems to change *my* shape. I go and order. Suzi checks her make-up. She

18

pulls faces at herself in a little mirror. *Like me in my room with the haka before I rang,* I think.

I come back with the food. Sit down. Stare across at her. She's picking bits of lettuce off the edge of her bun. She nibbles them and looks round. It's as if I'm not there. "Hey, Suzi," I say. "Thanks – you know – for coming." Naff, I know, but I have to start somewhere. She looks up. Her mouth is chewing lettuce like she's a rabbit. "I only came 'cos my mum wanted me to tidy up my room," she says. "So don't start getting ideas."

A real put-down, right? I do the only thing I can do. I shrug. "No worries," I tell her. "I was bored out of my head as well, once I finished knife practice."

"What?" she frowns.

I look at her. "Knife practice."

"What's that?"

I sigh. "Practice. With the knife. No use carrying a sharp if you're not sharp yourself." It comes out so cool, I wish I was someone else so I could admire me.

Suzi's looking at me now. "You saying you carry a *knife?*" she asks.

I nod. "Sure. Have for years. Got to, haven't you? Self defence."

"I ..." She looks at me. "I didn't think you'd carry *anything*, except maybe a spare nappy."

My turn to frown. "Shows how wrong you can be."

"Have you got it on you now?" she asks.

"'Course," I tell her. "Want to see?"

She nods. I take a quick look around, slip a hand in my jacket, take out my knife. "Don't let every skunk and his uncle see it." I slide it across the table to her.

She hides it with her bag, sits looking at it. "Where d'you get it?"

I grin. "There was a bit of a fight. Years back. Outside the footie stadium. Some bloke dropped it, running. I picked it up. Had it ever since." I'm amazed how all this bull comes pouring out of my mouth – I'm not even trying. And Suzi's lapping it up. She's like, "Have you stabbed anyone?"

I shake my head. "Not *stabbed*. You'll kill someone if you stab them. But I have cut one or two." What a lie. Biggest thing I've ever cut is a slice of bread.

Suzi slides the stiletto back to me, I drop it in my pocket. We eat. Lads sneak looks at Suzi. They wish they were me.

It's perfect, till Heston Weston sticks his beak in. He's a Year Ten. Not a Landshark, but a big, aggressive guy with a red, meaty face. I clocked him when Suzi and I came in. Him and his two mates. I've been keeping an

21

eye on them. I hope they don't want trouble. Some hope. Heston gets up and comes across as we finish eating. He leans across in front of me, puts his fists on the table and blocks me out. I can't even see Suzi now.

"Baby-sitting, eh, sweetheart?" Heston says to Suzi. She giggles.

"Something like that, Heston."

Heston. His mum and dad must be barmy. I mean, if your name's Weston you don't call your kid Heston, right? Heston Weston – it's like a name for a cartoon character.

Except he's not funny right now. I don't like trouble. Any other time, I'd maybe sit still and wait till Heston got bored dissing me and left. But this isn't any other time. I've just told Suzi what a hard guy I am, with a knife and everything. I can't just sit and take it, with my stiletto in my pocket. I'm scared, but there's no getting away from it – now's the time to try out one or two of those faces I practised in my mirror. I take a deep breath.

"Hey, Weston?" I murmur.

"Huh?" Heston turns round so as he can see me. "Did you say something, Titch?" he grunts at me.

I nod and slip my right hand inside my jacket. "Yeah. You're blocking my view. Back off." I hope he doesn't see how tense I am. He stays where he is, laughs. "You want me to back off, Titch, you're gonna have to make me." He turns back to Suzi. "Think the little guy'll make me, sweetheart?"

Suzi giggles. "Don't think so, Heston. He's all hat and no cattle, as the cowboys say."

"Is *that* what you think?" I jump up. My chair goes over. And there I am – crouched over the table, the knife held out in front of me. Can't really believe it.

"Hey, now, hold on," cries Weston. He backs away with his hands up, gawping at my blade. "I was having a laugh, that's all, there's no need ..."

I stare at him, then down at the knife, then at Suzi. It's unreal. Everyone in the place is looking at me. Heston Weston's almost messing himself. The manager's coming, with back-up. Suzi's looking up at me with big round eyes like I'm Brad Pitt. And none of it's real. Not me at all. It's like, the rubbish I talked earlier has come to life. And I'm trapped in it. Sam Brown – knifeman.

Mum'll *kill* me.

Chapter 5
Not the Real Me

"Take it easy, son." The manager stops just out of knife range. His two mates stop as well. "Put that thing away and leave. Do it now, and I won't call the police."

I crouch behind the knife and look all round. Everyone's staring at me. I hate it. All I want is for it to be over. But a part of me feels powerful. In control. All these people waiting to see what I'll do. *Me*, Sam Brown. No one's ever cared a stuff what I did. They care now, and a part of me likes the feeling. *Don't chuck it away*, goes a little voice inside my head. *Not just yet.* I point the knife at the manager and make a fake jabbing movement. He steps back. His back-up steps back too. I smile the tight smile I practised in the mirror.

"OK," I murmur. "We're leaving." I look all round the place, slowly. "No one moves till me and Suzi hit the street. Got it?"

Everyone nods. The manager looks at me. "It's cool, son. No one wants to mess with you. You won't be followed. Just put the knife away and go. I won't call the police."

I stare at him. "You're not as dumb as you look," I hear myself say. Only it's not me – not the real me. The real me feels like he's about to be sick. I give Suzi a quick look. "Come on."

How I make it out of the door I'll never know. I'm screaming inside – totally stressed out. Outside I hurry away, looking for a dark corner to fall apart in. Suzi trots beside me. Maybe I fooled her like everyone else. I hope so, and I don't want her with me in one minute's time when I totally lose it.

"Weston and his mates'll come looking, Suzi," I gasp as we go. "You better go."

She doesn't argue. Doesn't stop to give me a kiss on the cheek. Just makes a *huh!* sound, tosses her head and flounces off. I'm left all on my own. No one ever did that to Brad Pitt.

I find an alley that has wheelie-bins. I lean on the wall near the bins. I'm shaking so much I damn near cut myself as I put the knife away. Don't suppose *that* happens to Brad Pitt either. I lean there and take some deep breaths. Trying to stop the shakes.

All the time I'm listening for foot-steps. You bet I am. Heston Weston's foot-steps. I made him back off. He was scared and his mates saw. Scared of wimpy Sam Brown. His street cred's shot to bits. He'll want to get it back together. Only way to do that is to sort Sam Brown. Sort him once and for all. If

Heston finds me here, it won't be a picnic on the beach.

He doesn't come. I stay there ages. Leaning on the wall. I do deep breathing till the shakes die down. A DVD starts up inside my head. It's playing a movie of what happened at Pulse. I'm the star of the movie. See how I crouch behind my blade. Notice how cool I look. You don't know how my guts are churning. You don't know I'm hiding the shakes, that I'm thinking about my mum. The movie keeps replaying. Each time it plays I'm cooler, harder, more of a hero. Sam Brown, knifeman. Boyfriend of Suzi Pool.

I could nearly believe it myself.

"Nice time, love?" goes Mum when I walk in the house. What does she want me to say? "*Thanks, Mum, it was ace. I lost my rag down at Pulse, held everyone at knife-point. You and Dad would've been dead proud.*" Yeah, right.

What I *actually* do is mumble, "It was OK, I'm off to bed, g'night."

In my room I get a brilliant idea. I'll call Suzi. Check she got home all right. Tell her I did too. It's been special, see? A special evening in my life. I want to keep it going.

"Suzi?" I go.

"Oh, it's *you*," Suzi says. "I've just been talking about you."

"Yeah? Who to?" I ask.

"Cecil," Suzi says.

"Y-you're putting me on, right? That's a wind-up, isn't it?"

"No. Soon as I got in I called him, told him everything that went down tonight at Pulse. I wound *him* up – told him he needs to watch out."

"You *didn't*?"

"I did. He says he's not bothered but he is.
I can tell. He says he remembers you. From
primary school. You called him names. He's
been meaning to talk to you about it. I expect
he will now. G'night Sam. Sleep tight."

She laughs and cuts me off. *Sleep tight?*
I'll be lucky if I sleep at all and she knows it,
the twisted slag.

But I do sleep and I have this dream. I'm in
Sparrow Park at night. Alone. I never would
be of course, but you know how dreams are.
I'm not even nervous. I'm Sam the Wham. I'm
not kidding – in my dream, that's my nick-
name. Sam the Wham. I come to the swings.
The kiddies' play-ground. Cecil True is on a
swing. Heston Weston is pushing him. Heston
sees me coming and starts to scream. Cecil
yells at him, "*Push*, Heston, then jump on. He
can't touch us." I'm running towards the
swings. My knife's in my hand. I want to cut
them both. Heston gives the swing a mighty
shove, then jumps on. It's going so fast, it goes

right up over the bar, with Cecil sitting and Heston standing, gripping the chains. And it doesn't go over just once. It does it again and again, getting faster and faster. All I can see is a blur, like the propeller on a plane spinning round. I hear them laughing. I can't do anything. I'm forced to stand there like a total wuss. I hear a sound and look round. Suzi's at the top of the slide and she's watching me. She's pointing and laughing at me. "We don't date babies," she jeers.

That wakes me up.

Chapter 6
A Few More Miles of France

I lie awake after that, thinking. These are my thoughts.

Loads of guys were at Pulse.

They all saw me pull the knife.

What if one of 'em dobs me in? The manager said he wouldn't, but someone else might do it. Heston might do it for revenge. I could be stopped in the morning on my way to school. Searched. If the police catch me carrying a knife, they'll arrest me. I'll have to go to court. Mum and Dad will love that. Not.

So. Smart thing to do, leave the knife at home. Just for a day or two. If a copper stops me, I'm not carrying. I haven't got a knife. Never had one. Plus, if Suzi really *has* told Cecil, and he wants me to fight, I can't. Not got my weapon, see. It'll have to be some other time, OK?

I get out of bed. Tape the knife under my computer table. No one's going to find it there. I feel a bit better. Even manage a bit of kip before morning comes.

Thursday morning I walk to school without my knife. No copper stops me. I feel a bit let down. Cecil's not waiting for me by the gate either. Maybe Suzi was putting me on after all.

I tense up when the bell goes. What if some guy who was at Pulse has split on me to Mr Lewis? He's the head teacher. I can picture him walking in the classroom with a policeman. *"Come with me, Brown – the officer would like a word."*

That doesn't happen either. At morning break I corner Suzi in the yard. I'm like, *"Did you tell Cecil about me?"* I can't stand the suspense any longer, see? Suzi's with her two mates, Karen and Lauren. She looks at them and goes, "Did you hear something squeak?"

Lauren nods. "I think it was a shrimp, Suzi. There's one by your foot."

Suzi pretends to notice me for the first time. "So there is." She peers at me. "Did you say something, shrimp?"

I play along. "I asked if you really talked to Cecil last night."

"That's for me to know and you to find out," she says. Not a very good line – Suzi gets most of her lines off the soaps. "Come on, girls," she says. They leave me standing like a wuss, same as in my dream.

After lunch it's Citizenship. I go back to work in Jack Conyers' garden again. He brings me a cuppa, looks at me funny. "You weren't in Pulse last night by any chance?" he goes. I'm so gob-smacked I *nearly* forget to lie. Nearly. I shake my head. "No. I don't go in the week, Mr Conyers. Homework, you know."

He nods. "Ah. Only my lad's the manager, see? Says they had a spot of bother last night."

I look at him. "Your lad?"

"Aye," he says. "My son, Kevin. Told me some kid pulled a knife."

"A knife?" I goes. "Wow!"

"Yes, he says. "It was a commando knife."

"A *commando* knife?" I'm listening properly now. "You mean, like in World War Two, Mr Conyers?"

He nods. "Aye, lad, just like in World War Two. A real Fairbairn Sykes commando knife."

He looks right at me. "Not many of them around these days, I reckon."

I shake my head again. "No, I don't suppose there are, Mr Conyers." I'm tense. He knows something.

"Funny thing," he says. "I had mine till just the other day. Seems to have vanished now."

"Yours?" My mouth drops open. "You mean … you were a *commando*, Mr Conyers?"

He gives me a thin smile. "Oh, I wasn't *always* a silly old fart who can't dig his own bit of garden, Sam. I used to be Jacko Conyers – *Sergeant* Jacko Conyers, Commando."

All I can do is gawp at him. It's too weird – a coffin-dodger who was a hero. Why didn't he die back then when he was still a hero?

I wish I hadn't nicked his knife.

But there's nothing I can do about it right now, is there? Maybe I'll slip the stiletto back into his sad old drawer next Tuesday.

He's watching me. "My son told me what the boy looked like," he says. "Sounded a bit like you. That's why I asked."

"Right." I shake my head. "Like I said, mister, I don't go out in the week. Too much homework."

He doesn't push it any further. Goes in the house. I fetch the fork from the shed and dig up a few more miles of France.

Chapter 7
Surrounded

Friday I leave my knife at home again.
Well – no point carrying it when I'm giving it
back next Tuesday, is there?

It's been good, though. Word's got around.
Nobody bothered me yesterday. Nobody
bothers me today either. Heston Weston's got
a grudge. Cecil True always had. But they
avoid me. Stay away. I'm Sam the Wham. No
one *calls* me that – it was in my dream – but
they stay away.

It's now I make my big mistake. I should
leave it. Act cool, like nothing's changed. But

I don't. It feels so good, I have to brag. Lunch-time I share a table with Tim and six other guys. I says, "Notice how Cecil keeps his head down now I'm here?" Tim's like, "Ssssh!" The others don't say anything.

"Same goes for Heston Weston," I burble. "I faced him down, made him back off. You'd think he'd want to get even, but he keeps away." I do the tight smile. "He's not as dumb as he looks."

Like I said, I should have acted cool. There's a grass at my table and I don't know it. Nothing happens lunch-time or afternoon break. They wait till after school.

Twenty to four. Tim and me walking home. Tim's nervous. He hasn't got his fancy fisherman knife. Left it at home in case I get stopped when we're together. He's going on at me to be careful.

"Don't push your luck, Sam," he says. "I don't know why Weston hasn't flattened you.

Or what's stopping Cecil from shutting your mouth up. But I'd keep it shut anyway, if I were you. You might have fooled some guys, but you and I know you're not hard. You stir Cecil and his mates up, they'll have you for breakfast."

He's wrong, as it happens. They won't have me for breakfast. They'll have me for tea.

We're passing Sparrow Park. There's a low wall. Thick bushes. We hear a crashing, rustling noise. Guys come through the bushes and over the wall. Ten of them. It's the Landsharks. In seconds we're surrounded. There are other, normal people about, but they keep away.

"Now then, Brown." Cecil's tight smile is more scary than mine. "You know me, don't you? *Cess the Mess? Want to wrestle, Cecil?*" He lays his hand on my chest and gives me a shove. "Well – the answer's *yes*, Brown. I *do* want to wrestle. In fact I've waited years." He turns to Tim. "Get lost, kid – this has nothing to do with you."

Give Tim his due. He tries. "Sam's my mate," he says. "You don't run out on your mate."

Cecil looks at him. "*You* run out, or your blood does," he snarls. "You choose."

Tim gives me an awful look, then walks on. Can't blame him. Cecil turns back to me. "OK, Brown. Over the wall. *Now.*" I sit on the wall, swing my legs over. I don't even think about trying to run. Two Landsharks grab me. Throw me into the bushes. My face gets cut and scratched on twigs. I'm so scared I don't notice.

The same two guys grip my arms again and shove me along. There's a shelter in the park with a concrete floor. Kids use it in wet weather. Heston Weston's in there, grinning. So's Suzi. The two guys let go my arms. The gang makes a circle with me in the middle.

41

"OK, Brown," pants Cecil. "Let's see this famous knife."

I shake my head. "Haven't got it, Cecil. It's at home."

"Haven't got it – *sir*," he goes. "Respect me, Brown – say it."

"Haven't got it, sir," I murmur. Daren't do anything else.

"Louder!" he yells. "We didn't hear you."

"Haven't got it, SIR!" I shout. I'm nearly crying if you must know.

"That's a shame," goes Cecil. "I don't want to think about how our knife fight'll go, Brown. When one of us doesn't have a knife."

"I don't want to fight you," I croak. Suzi laughs.

"Huh?" Cecil frowns, looks round the circle. "Hear that, everyone? Hard man doesn't want to fight." He gives me a hard shove. I reel into Weston, who pushes me back in the middle.

"Well," says Cecil, "if you don't want to fight, we'll have to think up something you can do instead." He pretends to think. They're all staring at me, grinning and jeering. If I had the knife now, I swear I'd use it and die.

Cecil drives a fist into his palm. "*I* know!" he cries. "You can lick our *boots*, Brown. Or trainers, or shoes or whatever. Then we'll christen you *Boot Polish Brown*."

"Boot Polish Brown!" hoots Suzi. "It's the way you tell 'em, Cess!"

I have to take it. Just thinking about it now makes me want to cry. They all stand with one foot forward. Twelve shoes. I shuffle round the circle on my knees, licking. "Three licks per shoe," Cecil orders.

"Yes, sir," says I.

Twelve shoes. Twenty-four eyes looking down on me. Suzi's burn hottest.

It seems to go on forever. I boil with anger inside, but I don't let it show. Are they even going to let me go when I've finished? I don't know. I'm surrounded.

They do let me go. Or rather, they go. I stand up. My knees hurt and there's a nasty taste in my mouth. They walk away. No one says anything. No one looks back. It's the most horrible, lonely, *ashamed* feeling I've ever had.

I trail home. The replays are going round in my head. The replays show me as *they* saw me. As Suzi saw me. Not a shrimp. Not even a shrimp. A grub. Crawling at her feet, scared out of my head.

When I get home I don't know where to put myself. How can I show up at school Monday?

Or ever again. What a terrible, terrible thing it is they've done to me.

OK – I was a fool. Why didn't I keep my trap shut? Stupid. I admit it. But did I deserve to lick boots? *Did I?*

My head's so messed up I can't think. One thing's clear though. Crystal clear, and it's this –

Cecil True will die.

Chapter 8
Till the Day You Die

The week-end seems to go on forever. I stay in the house. But I can't stand to be with Mum and Dad. In one of the replays in my head movie, Mum and Dad are watching me crawl round that circle too. At least *that* didn't happen, I tell myself. Doesn't help much.

One thing will help. Cecil True, dead at my feet. Sounds sick I know, but nothing less will wash away my shame.

I make a plan. This is my plan.

Monday I'll go to school as always. It'll be hell. Word will have got round. My name will be known. My *new* name. Boot Polish Brown. Guys will call me that. Girls too. Especially Suzi. And I'll take it. Say nothing. Make everyone think I'm down. Finished. The end of Sam the Wham.

Tuesday I'll go to work for old Conyers as normal. I'll have his knife with me, but I won't give it back. What I'll do is, I'll offer to sort the shed. You can't move in there – it's like a tip. I've finished digging France, so he's bound to let me tackle it.

And here's the clever bit. While I'm in the shed, the old guy can't see me. If I slip away for a few minutes, he won't know. Cecil True's painting doors and window frames down the road on Tuesdays. I can cross a few back gardens and be with him in no time. He won't be expecting anything. I'll creep up on him, knife him and go back the same way. I'll leave the knife. No fingerprints, of course – I'm not daft. And if the police suspect me, Conyers will tell them *Sam was here when the lad was stabbed, doing out my shed. Sure? Of course I'm sure. My knife? It's vanished. I expect the killer pinched it. No, I never lock the shed.*

War hero, old Conyers. The coppers will believe him. And what's *really* sweet is, the kids'll know who wasted Cecil. They'll know it was me. It won't be Boot Polish Brown any more. It'll be Sam the Wham. Too hard to mess with, too smart to take the rap.

Good, eh?

Monday goes just like I knew it would. Wall-to-wall slagging. I don't mind. No one'll slag me off any more after Tuesday.

Tim doesn't slag. He's heard what they made me do. Feels bad. "I should've stuck with you," he says at morning break. I shake my head. "They'd have got *both* shoes cleaned instead of one, that's all." He knows I'm right.

The day passes slowly, but it passes. Tim and I walk home together, same as always.

Except we walk on the other side passing Sparrow Park. No one's there.

Tuesday morning I peel the tape off Jacko's knife, lift it off from under my computer table and slip it in my pocket. My plan's a good one and I know everything'll be all right. Still, now the day's here I feel a bit sick. My hands shake. A little voice in my head keeps asking stuff.

What if Conyers doesn't want the shed done out?

What if he brings you a cup of tea and you're not there?

What if Cecil has someone with him? Or he turns round just as you go to stab him and you miss?

And what about DNA?

I say "ta-ra" to Mum like I'm never going to see her again. Walking on Prince Street there's a lump in my throat and I talk to myself. I'm like, *You don't have to do this, Sam. Forget it, take the slagging. Slagging doesn't last forever.*

It's like I'm two guys. One guy's hoping Citizenship will be cancelled this afternoon. The other can't wait for it to start. I don't hear anything the teachers say. All I do is think about crossing the back gardens. Creeping up behind Cecil. Sticking the knife into him.

It's never going to happen. Two things mess it up. One weird, one stupid. Here's the weird one.

I do get to clear out the shed. I'm humping stuff out of the shed. Stacking it on the path. The old guy watches for a bit, then goes in the house. He comes out with tea. We stand drinking, looking at the stuff on the path. Most of it wants chucking. Suddenly he's like, "What's up, lad?"

"Huh?" I go. "*Nothing's* up. What d'you mean?"

He narrows his eyes. "You're tense, Sam. Jumpy. Something's up. Something you have to do."

I shake my head. "No." I try a grin. "Except get this lot sorted."

"Not that." He looks at me. "You're acting like my men did in the war before something big. Before a dodgy op. When they were scared but trying not to show it. What's the op, Sam?"

I want to yell, "*GET IN THE HOUSE! There's an op all right. Operation Stab Cecil, and I need to get on with it.*"

"Why don't you go in?" I ask. "I'll just get on and clear up this shed."

He shakes his head. "*Something's* up," he insists. "I'm never wrong."

"Well," I says, "you're wrong this time, Mr Conyers. I better crack on."

And then the stupid thing happens. I take off my jacket, chuck it at the shed door. It misses. Drops on the path. The knife falls out. "Ah," he goes. "I *knew* I was right. Come on."

He puts an arm round me. Steers me towards the house.

I'm like, "What you doing?"

"We're going to sit down," he says. "And I'm going to tell you a story."

It's crazy. We leave the knife lying there. I let him take me inside. A part of me wants to shake him off. Another part's glad. *My plan's messed up*, goes one part. *Thank God for that*, goes the other. We sit across from each other, in armchairs.

"It's 1941," he says. "France is thick with Nazi troops. Me and my men cross the Channel at night. We're going to blow up a dry

52

dock the German navy needs. We'll destroy other stuff while we're at it. We're out-numbered a hundred to one. Some of us will die. We know that, and we go anyway. It's what commandos do."

He looks at me. "The dagger you borrowed is part of my gear. It's for quick, silent killing. I've been trained to use it, I hope I'll never have to. But tonight I do. I have to do just that. There's a guard hut with a telephone inside and one German soldier. He's got the phone in his hand. He might be calling for back-up. I creep up behind him. There's a terrific racket going on outside. Gunfire. Explosions. He doesn't hear me. I throw an arm round his neck. Slip the knife in under his ribs. It finds his heart. He sighs and dies.

"He's just a young lad. I lower his body to the floor, and then I see what's on the table. He was writing home. The letter's there. He's not finished it. There's a snapshot too. An oldish couple, smiling at the camera. His mother and father, I expect. They look a lot like my own parents. They'll never get his letter now. Never see their precious boy again. Someone else's boy has taken him away from them."

Old Conyers looks at me. There are tears in his eyes. "I was a commando, Sam," he says. "A tough guy. But I couldn't get that snapshot out of my mind. *Still* can't, a lifetime after. That poor lad's mum and dad, smiling. It might easily have been *my* mum and dad."

He breaks off and stares at the floor. After a bit he says, "Everyone's someone's child, Sam. Even the people we hate. There's someone who'll grieve if they don't come home. If they *never* come home."

He stands up. Comes across. Grips my elbow. Looks hard at me. "Believe me, son," he murmurs, "you don't want to stab anyone. You do, and it'll haunt you till the day you die. I *know*."

Chapter 9
A Result

He's right, old Conyers. I think about it in bed, Tuesday night. Cecil's got a mum. A plain, fat mum in cheap kit. He has no dad, so Cecil's all she's got. He's a scrote, but I bet she loves him to bits.

I think about the knife as well. Conyers' knife. It was here, in this room. I played with it, like a kid with a toy sword. But it's *not* a toy. It went in a guy's heart and stopped it. Took him away from his parents. Messed up Conyers' life too. You can't feel big, touching a thing like that. You feel dirty.

Maybe that's why he hides it in a drawer, under all that rusty tat.

He doesn't dob me in, old Conyers. Even though I nicked his knife. I still do his garden, Tuesdays and Thursdays. By the time I've got it sorted, the slagging will have stopped. It's a bit better already. Mrs True's still got her boy, and Mrs Brown has me.

If that's not a result, I don't know what is.